God Made PUPPIES

by Marian Bennett

illustrated by Lorraine Arthur

Third Edition, 1994
Library of Congress Catalog Card No. 93-087237
© 1980, The Standard Publishing Company, Cincinnati, Ohio
A division of Standex International Corporation. Printed in U.S.A.

When God made puppies,
He made some very big,

and some very small.

He made some with long hair,

and some with almost no hair at all.

God gave some pups a long tail,

and others just some fluff.

While some pups may be fat and round,

this one's light as a puff.

Sometimes puppies can be very good,

and sometimes they are very bad!

Some puppies make us laugh,

while others look so sad.

Puppies come with a wagging tail,

and a cold, wet nose,

a little pink tongue,

and lots of toes!

Puppies like to bite and chew.

They may even like to chew on you!

Puppies need good food to eat,

water to drink,

and plenty of rest.

Puppies like all kinds of people—

moms and dads,

grandpas and grandmas—

and YOU the best!